ॐ

For my dad, who didn't let
life or death get him down
P. R.

For Tim—his father's son, as I am
D. P.

AUNT NANCY

～ and the ～

BOTHERSOME
VISITORS

PHYLLIS ROOT

ILLUSTRATED BY DAVID PARKINS

CANDLEWICK PRESS
CAMBRIDGE, MASSACHUSETTS

TABLE OF

CONTENTS

AUNT
NANCY
and
OLD MAN
TROUBLE

*A*unt Nancy should of knowed Old Man Trouble was in the neighborhood. Hadn't the spring out back gone and dried up this morning when she went to fill her water bucket?

And when she bent over the spring hole to see what had happened to the water, didn't her good-luck three-legged wooden buffalo nickel fall right out of her pocket *bloop* into the hole and no way to fetch it up again?

Here was the sun barely poking up in the sky, and already bad luck was hopping around like rabbits at a family reunion. Aunt Nancy should of knowed Old Man Trouble was around, all right.

But she didn't. When there came a knocking and a thumping on her door, what did she do but open it?

And there stood Old Man Trouble.

He was dressed in a long black coat, tall black hat, and shiny black shoes. He was swinging a silver-headed walking stick, and his pointy white teeth gleamed in his pointy black beard.

"Good day to you, ma'am," says Old Man Trouble, sliding one of those shiny black shoes into the doorway.

Quick as a whisker, Aunt Nancy slams the door and bolts it shut. She knows who Old Man Trouble is, all right, and no way is she going to let him in.

"Now, ma'am," says Old Man Trouble from the other side of the door, "you know it ain't no use to try and keep me out. Bolt your doors and windows shut, I'll just drift down your chimney. Plug up your chimney flue, I'll blow in through the cracks in the wall. Might as well open that door and let me in."

Old Man Trouble keeps knocking on the door. Soon or late, he knows, Aunt Nancy's gonna have to let him in.

Aunt Nancy, she sees the truth of that, but she knows a thing or two herself.

So when Old Man Trouble knocks again, Aunt Nancy winks at her cat, Ezekiel, opens the door wide, and says, "Might as well come on in."

Old Man Trouble steps in through the door as big as you please.

Ezekiel takes one look, and he hisses and howls and shoots out the door faster than a firecracker on the Fourth of July.

Fast as he is, Ezekiel isn't fast enough. The door nips shut on his tail, and he lights off for the nearest tree, yowling and howling. That's the kind of thing happens when Old Man Trouble comes around.

Aunt Nancy shuts the door and says, all polite, "Seat yourself and stay a spell."

"Don't mind if I do," says Old Man
Trouble. "I wouldn't say no to a cup of
tea, neither."

So Aunt Nancy puts the kettle on the
fire, and the next thing you know, the
fire's gone out, and when she blows on
the coals to start it up again, all she gets
is a face full of ashes. Out of the corner
of her eye she spies Old Man Trouble
grinning, but Aunt Nancy, she pretends
not to notice.

"Well, now, here's a blessing," says
Aunt Nancy. "The fire's gone out, and a

good thing too, a hot day like this. I'll just
get you a nice cool glass of water. There's
a drop or two left in the bucket."

Aunt Nancy reaches for a glass of
water, and don't that glass just kinda
jump sideways out of her fingers, splash
water down her front, and crash in a
million pieces on the floor?

Old Man Trouble's still grinning
through his beard, but Aunt Nancy, she
makes like she don't see him.

"Whoo-ee, don't that feel good," she says. "Cools me right off."

Old Man Trouble, he's not grinning quite so big as Aunt Nancy sweeps up the pieces.

"And there's another blessing," she says. "Didn't that glass have a crack in it, and me too cheap to throw it out? Now nobody'll get themselves cut trying to drink out of it."

Old Man Trouble, he's not grinning very much at all.

"And I'd get you another glass," says Aunt Nancy, "but the spring's gone dry this morning."

"Sit yourself down and rest, then," says Old Man Trouble.

Aunt Nancy starts to sit in a chair, when *creak, crack* the chair's lying on its side with one leg broken and *ka-thunk* Aunt Nancy's sitting on the floor.

"Now, ain't that a mercy," Aunt Nancy says, picking herself up. "Just when I was wondering where I was gonna get me some kindling wood."

Old Man Trouble stomps his silver-headed walking stick on the floor. Aunt Nancy can see he's mighty upset.

"Don't nothing bother you, ma'am?" says Old Man Trouble through his teeth.

"Not today it don't," says Aunt Nancy, fetching her rocking chair. "I just knowed it was my lucky day when I saw that spring dried up this morning. No more mud tracking up my floors. No more dampness aching in my bones."

Old Man Trouble starts to grin again.

"Reckon that'd be a real trouble to you, ma'am, if that spring come back again," he says.

"That it would," Aunt Nancy says. "But being as this is my lucky day, I'm not worried. You brought me nothing but good luck, and I thank you kindly."

"I'd better be getting along, then," says Old Man Trouble.

Aunt Nancy sees him to the door.

"Come again," she says, all polite.

"Oh, I will," says Old Man Trouble, stepping outside. "Say, ma'am," he asks, "do you hear water running somewhere?"

Aunt Nancy shakes her head. "Don't hear a thing," she says.

Old Man Trouble grins so hard, his face is about to split.

"You will, ma'am," he says. He tips his hat and sets off down the road, swinging his walking stick and humming to himself.

Aunt Nancy watches the back of Old Man Trouble away down the road.

All the while she's listening to the sweet sound of water gurgling, and she's grinning pretty big herself.

"Come on down, cat," she says to Ezekiel up in his tree. "You and me can sit and rock and rest a spell."

Aunt Nancy, she figures she earned it.

AUNT NANCY
and
COUSIN
LAZYBONES

*A*unt Nancy didn't turn any cartwheels when Cousin Lazybones come to visit.

She knowed he was so lazy even his shadow didn't get up and follow him around. But he was her fourth cousin three times removed on her great-aunt Hattie's sister's side, and family was family, so what could she do?

Ezekiel the cat knowed what to do. When Cousin Lazybones strolled in the door, Ezekiel strolled right on out and hid behind the woodshed. No way was he waiting around to wait on Cousin Lazybones.

"Hope you don't mind some company

for a month or two," says Cousin Lazybones. "When do we eat?"

"Soon as you feed the hens and gather me some eggs from the henhouse," says Aunt Nancy. She goes to get him a bucket of chicken feed.

"I'd be purely pleased to help out," says Cousin Lazybones. "But it don't make sense to go looking for eggs when the eggs can come looking for you."

So don't he just start throwing chicken feed on Aunt Nancy's floor and calling out, "Here, chick-chick-chick-chick-chick"?

And don't the chickens just come cackling and clucking through the doorway, chicken fleas, feathers, and all?

"Now, ain't that an idea?" says Aunt Nancy. "Why didn't I think of that? Course, somebody's gonna have to clean up after them chickens, and it can't be me. I got to get lunch on the table."

"Shoo, shoo!" Cousin Lazybones flaps at the chickens. "Reckon I'll go gather the eggs after all. I got to rest up a bit first, though. My knees is a bit wobbly from all this work."

So off Cousin Lazybones heads for Aunt Nancy's rocking chair, and off Aunt Nancy heads to the woodstove to finish the fixings for lunch. Pretty soon Aunt Nancy is knee-deep in work, and Cousin Lazybones is sawing down a whole forest of trees in his sleep.

He does get up long enough to eat seventeen helpings of lunch, howsoever.

"I'd take it kindly if you fetched me some water from the spring for washing up," Aunt Nancy says as she's clearing the table.

"I'd be tickled purple to lend a hand,"

says Cousin Lazybones. "I'll just take this-here bucket and set it right outside the door. Reckon it'll rain before long and fill it up."

"Now, ain't that an idea?" says Aunt Nancy. "Why didn't I think of that? Course, if it don't rain by evening, there won't be any clean pots to cook supper in. I'd go get the water myself, but I got to be ironing the bedsheets."

So off Cousin Lazybones goes with the water bucket. He's near as far as the door when he hollers, "Ow-w-w-w-w!" and gets all bent over.

"Just a little hitch in my git-along," he tells Aunt Nancy. "Right here . . . or maybe here. I'll fetch the water soon as I rest up a bit."

So off he heads to rest his git-along in the rocking chair and saw down another couple of forests.

He does get up long enough to eat twenty-two helpings of supper, howsoever.

Aunt Nancy's ready for him this time. "Water's already heating on the stove," she says. "I wouldn't mind a hand with the washing up if your git-along's not too hitched."

"I'd be pleased as petunias to help," says Cousin Lazybones. "These-here dishes ain't but half dirty. I'll just turn them over so's we can use the other side for breakfast."

"Now, ain't that an idea?" says Aunt Nancy. "Why didn't I think of that? Course, I don't know what we're gonna do when both sides is dirty."

"Reckon then it'll be your turn to wash," says Cousin Lazybones. "Right now I'm plumb wore out from all this thinking. I feel a rest coming on."

And off he heads for Aunt Nancy's rocking chair to clear-cut another couple acres of trees until time for bed.

Now, Aunt Nancy had more brains than God gave a whole flock of geese. She could see the way things was gonna go with Cousin Lazybones around. She knowed who'd be doing all the work and who'd be doing all the resting up.

"Can't turn him out," Aunt Nancy tells Ezekiel as she empties the dishwater behind the woodshed. "Family is family. But enough is enough."

That night Aunt Nancy tidies up so good even a cockroach would starve to death.

And next morning don't she just stay in bed, even when the sun is hanging halfway up the sky?

Along about noon Cousin Lazybones

rolls out of bed. But the table is as bare as a possum's tail.

"Aunt Nancy?" calls Cousin Lazy-bones, all pitiful-like. "When do we eat?"

Aunt Nancy moans and hobbles to her rocking chair.

"Reckon you'll have to fix yourself something," she groans. "I woke up this morning with a bone in my leg, so's I can hardly walk. Not only that, I got a chest full of breath and such a terrible mess of brains in my head I can't hardly think.

This being my spring-cleaning day, it's lucky for me you're here to help, you having two good legs and a head full of good ideas. After you cook and wash up, you can sweep the floor and shake out the rugs—"

Cousin Lazybones jumps like a frog in a frying pan. "I just remembered something," he says.

"—and scrub the stove and wash the windows—"

"I think Uncle Wilbur's looking for me to stop in and visit him soon," says Cousin Lazybones.

"—and dust the ceiling and polish the lamp chimney and—"

"Matter of fact, I believe I'm late," says Cousin Lazybones.

He hightails it out the door like a chicken at a fox convention. Aunt Nancy watches him down the road, till he's no bigger than a dust ball.

"Come on out, cat," she calls to Ezekiel, behind the woodshed. "With this bone in my leg and this breath in my chest and all these brains in my head today, I can't think of but one thing to do."

Ezekiel pokes his head out. What does he see but Aunt Nancy whooping and hollering and turning cartwheels all the way around the yard?

AUNT
NANCY
and
OLD
WOEFUL

*L*ucky for Aunt Nancy her head wasn't up on her shoulders just to keep her ears from fighting with each other. And didn't Aunt Nancy need all the brains she could get the day Old Woeful come down the road?

Aunt Nancy could see Old Woeful coming a long ways off. Maybe it was on account of Old Woeful's long dark shadow stretching out in front of her. Maybe it was the little rain cloud hanging over Old Woeful's head. Maybe it was her voice moaning "Woe, woe, woe" like a lost dog in a graveyard. Aunt Nancy saw Old Woeful coming, all right. Wasn't much she could do about it, though, just keep on hoeing her pea patch.

Ezekiel the cat knowed what to do. He crawled under the rhubarb leaves and put his paws over his ears.

Just in time, too. Here comes Old Woeful dumping doom and gloom around her.

"Ain't no use bothering with that garden," grumbles Old Woeful before Aunt Nancy can so much as say good morning. "Bound to rain before long and wash it all away."

Aunt Nancy looks up at the sky. The sun's shining like a bright copper pot, and the only cloud around is the one hanging over Old Woeful's sorry head.

"You'll excuse me, then, if I don't stop to chitchat with all the work I got to do before the rain comes," Aunt Nancy says. "My peas surely could do with a little shower."

"Won't be no little shower," warns Old Woeful. "Bound to come down a frog-choker and drown us all in our beds."

Old Woeful's cloud dribbles a little just thinking about all that wet. Ezekiel slinks farther under the rhubarb leaves.

"If it's fixing to pour, I'd best pick my bimbleberries before they're under water," says Aunt Nancy. "I got a hankering for some bimbleberry pie. Been nice talking to you." And off Aunt Nancy hustles to her bimbleberry bushes.

Aunt Nancy's picking bimbleberries six ways to Sunday when she hears *drizzle, drizzle, drizzle,* and here comes Old Woeful.

"Might as well plan your own funeral as pick bimbleberries," Old Woeful gripes. "There ain't nothing bears love more than bimbleberries. One whiff of your pie, and they'll be knocking on the door like the Fuller brush salesman. You open the door to see who's knocking, and the bears eat you up right along with your pie."

Old Woeful's cloud shudders and shoots out a little bolt of lightning.

Aunt Nancy sets down her basket of bimbleberries.

"If it won't make no never mind to pick berries," she says, "maybe I should get on with mucking out the chicken coop. Might be the smell will keep the bears away. Don't let the gate smack you on the way out, now." And off Aunt Nancy heads to the chicken coop.

Old Woeful, she wouldn't know a hint if it bit her on the behind, and pretty soon *drizzle, drizzle, drizzle,* she's standing right alongside Aunt Nancy.

"No use messing with mucking," warns Old Woeful, all doleful-like. "Sure as shooting, you'll catch your death of muckitis. Horrible way to go."

In all her years of mucking, Aunt Nancy ain't never heard of muckitis, but she does know Old Woeful will go on grousing till the hens come home to sleep. "Well, if there's no sense in hoeing or berry picking or chicken-coop mucking, I guess there's only one thing to do," says Aunt Nancy.

She finds a nice patch of dirt and commences to dig.

"Reckon I'd better keep you company while you dig," says Old Woeful. "Likely you'll be digging up a mess of rattlesnakes or some such."

"Suit yourself," says Aunt Nancy. "You just sit right over there by my pea patch so I don't get no dirt on you."

Old Woeful plops her pitiful self down like she's fixing to take root. Her cloud settles in and starts some serious raining all over Aunt Nancy's pea patch. Every so often the cloud spits a little shower at Ezekiel.

After a spell, Old Woeful asks, "What're you digging for, anyway?" Aunt Nancy makes like she don't hear her.

"Not a posy bed, is it?" says Old Woeful. "Bees is bound to come from miles around and buzz you all to death."

"Ain't a posy bed," says Aunt Nancy.

"Ain't fishing worms, is it? Nasty things can kill you with a case of the slimes."

Aunt Nancy shakes her head and keeps digging.

"Best not be a pumpkin patch. I hear tell a farmer got tangled in his own pumpkin vines and starved hisself to death."

"Ain't a pumpkin patch," says Aunt Nancy.

"Well, then," says Old Woeful, "what are you digging anyways?"

Aunt Nancy leans on her shovel. "The way I figure things," she says, "I'm either gonna drown in my bed or get et up by

bears. That's if I don't die of muckitis or get buzzed or slimed or tangled to death. Any way you look at it, I'm due to be pushing up petunias before long, so I reckon it's only good manners to dig my grave now and save you the trouble of digging it later. While I'm at it, I'd be right happy to dig yours for you, too."

Old Woeful's eyes get big as tombstones. "Aunt Nancy, you are about the gloomiest person I ever laid eyes on," she says. "I got to be getting along before you give me a serious case of the dismals." And she skedaddles down the road so fast her rain cloud has to hustle to keep up with her.

"Come on out and take a gander, Ezekiel," says Aunt Nancy.

"My potato patch is dug, there's plenty of fishing worms for catching supper, and since I don't have to water my pea patch no more, I got time to bake us a bimbleberry pie." Aunt Nancy, she reckons she might even pick some posies to put on the table.

AUNT
NANCY
and
MISTER
DEATH

Never was nobody as tricksy as Aunt Nancy. Folks say she even outsmarted Mister Death hisself when he come down the road looking for her.

He come right up into her yard with his shirtfront all ruffly white and a big, bright watch chain across his middle. Aunt Nancy, she takes one look and knows she's gonna need every trick she's ever learned and a few she hasn't to outsmart Mister Death.

Ezekiel the cat, he takes one look and all his hair stands on end, big as a chimney brush.

Aunt Nancy, she keeps right on sweeping her porch.

"Aunt Nancy," says Mister Death, all solemn and churchlike, "your time is come."

"I can't go yet," says Aunt Nancy. "I got me a heap of housecleaning to do."

"No time for that," says Mister Death, checking his shiny gold watch.

"What would the neighbors say with me dead and my floor all dirty?" says Aunt Nancy. "I hear tell you're a bighearted feller. Just let me scrub it once before I go."

Mister Death, he preens hisself a little. Not too many folks appreciate his finer points.

"I reckon I can spare you a minute or two," he says.

"You just sit yourself down and promise not to move till the floor's clean," Aunt Nancy says. "A hardworking feller like you deserves a rest."

So Mister Death, he sits hisself down and promises to stay there till Aunt Nancy's floor is clean. And Aunt Nancy, she sits herself down and commences to rock.

"Aunt Nancy, you got no time to be rocking," says Mister Death. "How long you think I'm gonna sit here?"

"Till my floor is clean," Aunt Nancy says. "A promise is a promise, and I reckon I can live with a dirty floor a mighty long time."

Mister Death, he fumes and he fusses, but he sees he's been tricked pretty good. Seems like he's gonna be sitting in that chair till the cows come to dinner.

"Look here," says Mister Death, "you let me up and I'll let you have one more year."

Aunt Nancy, she sees that's the best she's gonna get. And a year seems like a mighty long, sweet time.

But before you know it, here's another year rolled around with good times and hard times, and here's Mister Death coming back down the road to Aunt Nancy's house.

Ezekiel hightails it into the house and up the chimney. He figures he's gonna miss Aunt Nancy something awful, but no way is he planning on keeping her company.

"Aunt Nancy, your time is come," says Mister Death. "And you're not tricking me into no promises this time, neither."

"I'm coming," says Aunt Nancy. "But there ain't nobody to milk my cow when I'm gone. I'm gonna have to bring her along with me."

"I ain't got no use for a cow," says Mister Death.

"If the cow don't go, I don't go," says Aunt Nancy.

Mister Death, he's getting edgy on account of he has a lot of important appointments that day. He can see Aunt

Nancy is one mighty stubborn woman, and it's gonna be quicker to give in than it is to argue.

"Bring your cow," he snaps.

"And somebody's got to carry her," Aunt Nancy says. "She's too tuckered out to walk. You look like a mighty strong feller to me."

Mister Death, he flexes a muscle or two. He reckons maybe he is a pretty fine figure of a man. So he picks up the cow and heads off down the road with Aunt Nancy trailing along behind.

Strong   or   not,   before   long   he's

drooping and dragging. Besides which, he can hear by his shiny gold watch that time is ticking away.

"Aunt Nancy," says Mister Death. "I can't carry this cow no farther."

"Now, what would folks say if word got around you was too weak to carry off a cow?" asks Aunt Nancy. "Who'd come with you then?"

Mister Death, he can see if he's not careful, his reputation is gonna be ruined and he'll be down in the unemployment line. He sizzles and he simmers, but he can see he's been tricked again.

"One more year," he snarls. "But that's all you get."

"Suits me fine," says Aunt Nancy. "Now, who's gonna carry this cow back home?"

Well, one more year comes around, and before you know it, so does Mister Death.

Ezekiel's ready for him this time. He rolls over and sticks his legs up in the air.

 Mister Death can't have no use for a cat that's already dead.

"Aunt Nancy, your time is up," says Mister Death. "I ain't standing for no tricks this time, neither."

"Just let me get my lantern," says Aunt Nancy. "I hear it's mighty dark where we're going."

"Aunt Nancy, it's broad daylight," says Mister Death.

"I'm going with my lantern, or I'm not going at all," says Aunt Nancy.

Mister Death, he remembers it's no use arguing with Aunt Nancy. And besides, he can see by his watch that he's getting behind again.

Pretty soon here comes Aunt Nancy with her lantern lit, and she sets off down the road with Mister Death.

They haven't gone far before she's shivering and shaking.

Pretty soon she's twitching and trembling.

"Aunt Nancy, what are you carrying on so for?" says Mister Death.

"I'm so scared, my bones are shaking,"

moans Aunt Nancy. "I can't hardly hold on to this-here lantern. Folks say you're a mighty kind soul. Reckon you could carry it for me?"

Mister Death, he sighs once or twice. But ain't nobody called him kind in a century or so, and Aunt Nancy looks so pitiful, he can't refuse.

Soon as he's holding the lantern Aunt Nancy moans louder yet.

"It's so dark!" she wails.

Lickety-split she turns up the lantern wick. Mister Death's ruffly shirt starts to smoking like a cracked chimney. Screeching and howling, he heads for the pond.

And when he comes up for air, his ruffly white shirt is all ruined, and his shiny gold watch has done ticked its last.

"Doggone it, Aunt Nancy," snaps Mister Death. "I'm never coming near you again as long as I live."

"Suits me fine," says Aunt Nancy, and off she heads to feed Ezekiel his supper.

❧

Some folks say Mister Death finally did get hold of Aunt Nancy. Sneaked up behind her when she wasn't looking and took her away.

But you and me, we know better. Nobody ever got the best of Aunt Nancy, and nobody ever will.

The first two stories in this book were previously
published individually by Candlewick Press:

Aunt Nancy and Old Man Trouble
Text copyright © 1996 by Phyllis Root
Illustrations copyright © 1996 by David Parkins

Aunt Nancy and Cousin Lazybones
Text copyright © 1996 by Phyllis Root
Illustrations copyright © 1996 by David Parkins

—

Aunt Nancy and Old Woeful and *Aunt Nancy and Mister Death*
Text copyright © 2007 by Phyllis Root
Illustrations copyright © 2007 by David Parkins

First edition 2007

Library of Congress Cataloging-in-Publication Data is available.

Library of Congress Catalog Card Number pending

ISBN 978-0-7636-3074-4

2 4 6 8 10 9 7 5 3 1

Printed in Singapore

This book was typeset in Bembo Educational.
The full-color illustrations were done in oil and acrylic,
and the black-and-white illustrations were done in ink.

Candlewick Press
2067 Massachusetts Avenue
Cambridge, Massachusetts 02140

visit us at www.candlewick.com